SOFIA MARTINEZ

My Family
Adventure

by Jacqueline Jules

illustrated by Kim Smith

PICTURE WINDOW
a capstone imprint

Sofia Martinez is published by
Picture Window Books, a Capstone Imprint
1710 Roe Crest Drive
North Mankato, MN 56003
www.capstoneyoungreaders.com

Copyright © 2015 by Picture Window Books

Library of Congress Cataloging-in-
Publication data is available on the
Library of Congress website

ISBN 978-1-4795-5790-5 (pbk.)

Summary: Sofia Martinez has a big
personality and big plans, which makes
every day memorable. Between her sisters
and cousins, her family is the focus of her
many adventures. From taking school
pictures to doing chores, this 7-year-old
knows how to make every moment count.
Sofia loves her family and loves her life.
What could be better?

Designer: Kay Fraser

Printed in the United States of America in
North Mankato, Minnesota.
082019   000095

TABLE OF CONTENTS

Picture Perfect

CHAPTER 1

Picture Trick

Sofia stared at the school pictures from last year. They were lined up on top of the piano.

"I knew it!" Sofia said. "We are all wearing blue!"

All three Martinez sisters had
long dark hair, brown eyes, and a
few freckles. Sofia was the youngest
sister. Luisa was in the middle.
Elena was the oldest.

Everyone said the girls looked alike. This annoyed Sofia. She wanted to stand out.

"I have a plan," Sofia said.

Sofia put her picture in Elena's frame. She put Elena's picture in her frame.

"¡Perfecto!" Sofia said.

Just then, her mom walked into the living room.

"¡Mira!" Sofia said. "We all

wore blue last year."

"How cute," Mamá said with

a smile.

That was not what Sofia wanted
to hear. She waited for her mom to
see the switch. She didn't notice.

Sofia folded her arms. She was going to have to work harder to get someone to notice her picture trick.

CHAPTER 2

The Crazy Bow

That night all the family came for dinner. Sofia loved seeing her cousins, especially baby Mariela.

Mariela wore a big bow in her hair. Everyone kept talking about that crazy bow.

"She looks like a birthday

present!" Papá laughed.

Abuela couldn't stop smiling.

"Niña hermosa."

Tío Miguel took a bunch of pictures and showed everyone.

Baby Mariela was hogging all the attention. Sofia knew she had to get her family closer to the piano. Then they would see the picture switch.

"¿Mamá?" Sofia asked. "Will you play a song for us?"

"I would love to," Mamá said.

Mamá was a piano teacher. She knew lots of songs, and the Martinez family loved to sing.

Everyone gathered around the piano and sang and sang. Sofia waited and waited. Nobody noticed the picture switch.

Sofia did not feel like singing anymore. She went and sat down on the couch and pouted. Her papá followed her.

"¿Qué pasa?" Papá asked

Sofia. "You are always the loudest

singer in our group."

"Not tonight," Sofia said. "I am too sad to sing."

"¿Por qué?" Papá asked.

"No one ever notices me," Sofia said sadly.

"My sweet Sofia," Papá said. "There are a lot of people here. Everyone can't always pay attention to you."

"Why not? I want to stand out!" Sofia said.

Papá laughed. "Like baby Mariela and that giant bow?"

"¡Exactamente!" Sofia said.

Sofia felt better. Thanks to Papá,
she had a new idea.

She gave her papá a big hug

and went back to the piano to sing.

CHAPTER 3

The New Picture

On Monday morning, Sofia got up early. It was picture day. She needed her cousin Hector's help before pictures. She ran across the yard to talk to him. They didn't have much time.

"I can help you, but we have to
be quiet," Hector said.

Hector and Sofia tiptoed into
baby Mariela's room.

"Don't forget to give this back," he whispered. "It's my mom's favorite one."

"Gracias, Hector," Sofia said.

She ran back home to finish getting ready. It was a big day, and she wanted everything to be perfect. Sofia couldn't wait to take her school picture this year!

* * *

The day school pictures were delivered, Sofia ran home. Her picture was perfect!

Mamá and Tía Carmen were talking in the kitchen.

Sofia rushed past them.

"What's the big hurry, Sofia?"

Mamá asked.

Sofia went straight to her frame on the piano. She slipped her new school picture inside.

She jumped when Mamá and Tía Carmen walked in. Her sisters were right behind them.

"What do you think?" Sofia

asked. She was very proud.

When her sisters saw the

picture, they started laughing.

But Sofia didn't care.

"Oh, Sofia!" Mamá said, smiling. "¡Muy hermosa!"

"How did you get baby Mariela's bow?" Tía Carmen asked.

"Hector helped me," Sofia said. "No te preocupes. I already put it back in its spot."

"Why did you wear the bow, Sofia?" Mamá asked.

Sofia told them how she had mixed up the old school pictures.

"No one even noticed," Sofia said, frowning. "I looked too much like Elena."

"Not any more," Mamá said.

"¡Yo sé!" Sofia giggled. "Now my picture is special."

"It always was," Mamá said. "All three of my girls are special."

She put her arms out to give Sofia, Luisa, and Elena a big hug.

"Te quiero, Mamá," Sofia said.

"Te quiero, Sofia," Mamá said.

Abuela's Birthday

CHAPTER 1

The Piñata

Sofia carried a big bag across the yard to her cousins' house. The bag was very special. It held everything they needed to make a piñata for Abuela.

"Do you really think Abuela will like this?" Hector asked. "Isn't she too old for a piñata?"

"No one is too old for a fun birthday party," Sofia said.

Sofia pulled newspapers,

balloons, and paint from the bag.

Bella the cat came over and tried

to get in the bag.

"Silly gata!" Sofia said. "There is nothing here for you."

"What do we do first, Sofia?" Hector asked.

"That's easy. We tear the paper into strips," Sofia said.

She handed newspaper to Manuel, Alonzo, and Hector. Together, they made a big pile of paper strips on the kitchen floor.

"¡Perfecto! Now we need flour
and water to mix for the paste,"
Sofia said.

"Here's the flour," Hector said.
"It's really heavy. ¡Ayúdame!"

Sofia shook her head. She could
not help him. She was too busy
blowing up a balloon for the middle
of the piñata.

Hector started to pour the flour into a bowl by himself.

POP! Sofia's balloon broke.

Hector jumped and dropped the entire bag of flour. It landed right on top of Bella.

"Oh, no!" he yelled.

CHAPTER 2

Cat Chaos

Before they could stop her, Bella ran through the big pile of newspaper strips. She was getting flour all over! Little pieces of paper flew everywhere, too. It was a big disaster.

"Grab her!" Sofia yelled.

They reached for Bella over and over. But she slipped through their hands in a cloud of flour dust every time they got close.

"Mamá is going to be really mad," Alonzo said.

They had to get Bella cleaned up before they got in trouble.

"Where are the kitty treats?" Sofia asked.

Hector grabbed a little pink bag
from the cabinet. He quickly gave
it to Sofia.

"Ven aquí, gata," Sofia said quietly as she waved a treat in the air.

Sofia slowly walked toward the bathroom. The hungry cat followed her right in.

Bella left a trail of white paw prints all over. But that was a problem for later.

"¡Rápido! Close the door," Sofia said to Hector.

Sofia filled the tub with water.

Bella jumped into Hector's arms.

"What are we going to do?"

Hector asked. "Cats don't like to

take baths."

Sofia picked up a big brush by the sink.

"Does she like this?" she asked.

"¡Sí!" Hector said. "Mamá brushes her once a week."

Hector and Sofia sat down on the floor. They took turns gently brushing Bella.

Alonzo and Manuel banged on the bathroom door. "Let us in!"

All the noise woke Tía Carmen from her nap.

"¿Qué pasa?" Tía Carmen yelled from the kitchen.

"Oh, no! We're in big trouble," said Hector.

CHAPTER 3

The Big Mess

Sofia and the boys ran to the kitchen. Flour, newspaper strips, and kitty tracks covered the floor. Tía Carmen did not look happy. And she hadn't even seen the bathroom yet!

"What a disaster!" she said.

"What were you kids doing?"

Sofia told Tía Carmen that they

were trying to make a piñata.

"That is a nice idea, but next time you need to ask first," Tía Carmen said. "And now you have to clean up."

Sofia and her cousins cleaned everything. When they were done, Sofia asked Tía Carmen for more newspaper and flour.

"¿Para qué?" Tía Carmen asked, looking confused.

"A new piñata for Abuela!"

Sofia said.

Tía Carmen laughed. "Silly

Sofia. I don't think so. You'll just

make another mess."

"No, we won't," Sofia said.

"I promise!"

"We really want Abuela to have

a piñata for her birthday," Alonzo

said. "Please?"

"¿Por favor?" Hector said.

Tía Carmen sighed.

"Okay, okay. Grab all the stuff you need, and go out on the patio," she said. "I'll keep Bella inside."

"Hooray!" Sofia yelled.

This time, Tía Carmen helped make the paste mixture. No flour spilled, and all the paper strips were pasted on the balloon. Not one got in the house.

Sofia's big sisters, Luisa and
Elena, came over to help paint
the piñata.

"We need to put candy inside," Elena said.

"Everybody gets candy," Sofia said. "Let's do something more unique for Abuela."

"Something she loves," Hector said. "Like playing cards."

It was true. Abuela loved card games. All the grandchildren spent hours at her house playing Go Fish and Old Maid.

"Great idea!" Sofia said. "She will love it! This will be one party she will never forget."

* * *

On the day of the party, Tío Miguel hung the piñata on a tree limb. Abuela put on the blindfold and swung the stick first. Then everybody else took turns.

Abuela laughed when Sofia finally broke the piñata and the cards spilled out.

"Playing cards! ¡Gracias!" Abuela said. "I love my party!"

"And we love you," Sofia said.

"¡Feliz cumpleaños, Abuela!"

The Missing Mouse

CHAPTER 1

Meet Snowflake

Sofia heard a knock at the door and rushed to answer it. It was Albert. He came every Friday afternoon to take piano lessons with Sofia's mom.

Today Albert had a shoe box with him. Sofia knew exactly what was in it.

"Hola, Sofia," Albert said.

"¡Hola! Is that Snowflake?"
Sofia asked.

"¡Sí!" Albert said proudly. "I'm
the very first person to take care of
our class pet."

"You are so lucky," Sofia said.

"But we have a problem."

"What?" Albert asked.

"Fur makes Mamá sneeze," Sofia said.

"Really?" Albert asked.

"Sí," Sofia said. "Our cat had to move to a new house."

"What should I do?" Albert asked. "My piano lesson starts in a few minutes!"

"Don't worry," Sofia said. "I'll take care of Snowflake."

"Are you sure?" Albert asked, looking worried.

"No hay problema," Sofia said,

smiling.

Albert wasn't so sure, but he

didn't have any other options.

"Snowflake likes to escape. Please don't let him run away," Albert said.

"Got it," Sofia said.

Sofia took the box downstairs. Luisa and Elena, Sofia's older sisters, were watching TV.

"¿Qué tienes?" Luisa asked.

"A mouse," Sofia said. "His name is Snowflake."

"Whose is it?" Luisa asked.

"It is Albert's class pet," Sofia

said. Luisa looked impressed. Elena

looked bored.

"I think Snowflake wants to see what we are watching," Sofia said.

She slowly lifted the lid. The white mouse stood up on his back legs. He squeaked.

"How cute!" Sofia laughed.

"He is cute!" Luisa agreed.

"Please be quiet," Elena said. "I'm trying to watch my show."

"Okay, okay," Sofia said.

Sofia was just about to close the lid when Snowflake jumped out of the box.

"NO!" Sofia screamed.

CHAPTER 2

The Lost Mouse

Snowflake ran across the floor and under the big chair.

"Aaahhh!" her sisters screamed.

"¡Ayúdame!" Sofia cried.

"No way!" Elena shouted. "I'm telling Mamá!"

"You can't!" Luisa said.

The Martinez sisters knew better

than to bother Mamá when she was

teaching piano lessons.

"We should call Abuela," Sofia decided. "She always knows how to fix things."

"Well, you better do something fast," Elena said. "We don't have much time."

Sofia ran across the room to get the phone. Sofia listened carefully for several minutes.

Then she thanked her abuela and hung up.

"Good news! All we need is a bucket," Sofia announced.

"¿Para qué?" Elena asked.

"To catch Snowflake," Sofia said. "It should be pretty easy."

"Mamá has one in the laundry room," Luisa said. "I'll get it."

When Luisa came back, the girls stared at the bucket.

"Abuela says to put food for the mouse inside," Sofia said.

"Okay. What do mice eat?" Luisa asked.

"Cheese," Elena said.

"That is a problem," Luisa said, pointing at the ceiling. "The cheese is upstairs in the kitchen."

The sounds of Albert on the piano came through. There was no way they could get to the kitchen without being noticed.

"That is not going to work," Elena said.

"No te preocupes. I'll go
across the yard to Tía Carmen's,"
Sofia said. "¡Adiós!"

CHAPTER 3

The Mouse Trap

A few minutes later, Sofia was back with her cousin Hector.

"I'm back, and I brought help," she said proudly.

"I really just want to see the mouse," Hector said.

"First we have to catch him," Elena said. "Did you bring some cheese?"

"No," Hector said. "We are out of cheese."

"We brought peanut butter instead," Sofia said.

"Peanut butter?" Elena said.

"Mamá said mice like it as much as cheese," Hector added.

Sofia smeared peanut butter inside the bucket. Then she put the bucket near the big chair.

"The bucket is too tall for a mouse," Hector said.

"We need stairs," Sofia said. "Grab my blocks, Hector."

Sofia and Hector started building the stairs. They worked fast.

Soon the bucket trap was ready.

Sofia, Luisa, Elena, and Hector

hid near the chair and watched.

No one made a sound. They saw

Snowflake run out.

Snowflake stood on his back
legs and sniffed. He began to climb.
Then they heard the mouse plop in
the bucket.

"¡Lo hicimos!" Sofia shouted.

"Our plan worked!"

Everybody cheered.

Just then, Albert opened the door. "Where's Snowflake?"

"¡Aquí!" Sofia proudly pointed at the bucket.

Albert scooped up the mouse. "You said you wouldn't let him run away."

"¡Yo sé! He didn't run away," Sofia said. "He had an adventure."

"So did we," Elena said.

Snowflake squeaked, and

everybody laughed — even Albert.

Spanish Glossary

abuela — grandma

adios — goodbye

aquí — here

ayúdame — help me

exactamente — exactly

feliz cumpleaños — happy birthday

gata — female cat

gracias — thank you

hola — hello

lo hicimos — we did it

mamá — mom

mira — look

muy hermosa — very beautiful

niña hermosa — beautiful little girl

no hay problema — no problem

no te preocupes — don't worry

papá — dad

para qué — for what

perfecto — perfect

por favor — please

por qué — how come

qué pasa — what's wrong

qué tienes — what do you have

rápido — quick

sí — yes

te quiero — I love you

tía — aunt

tío — uncle

ven aquí — come here

yo sé — I know

About the Author

Jacqueline Jules is the award-winning author of twenty-five children's books, including *No English* (2012 Forward National Literature Award), *Zapato Power: Freddie Ramos Takes Off* (2010 CYBILS Literary Award, Maryland Blue Crab Young Reader Honor Award, and ALSC Great Early Elementary Reads), and *Freddie Ramos Makes a Splash* (named on 2013 List of Best Children's Books of the Year by Bank Street College Committee).

When not reading, writing, or teaching, Jacqueline enjoys time with her family in Northern Virginia.

About the Illustrator

Kim Smith has worked in magazines, advertising, animation, and children's gaming. She studied illustration at the Alberta College of Art and Design in Calgary, Alberta.

Kim is the illustrator of the upcoming middle-grade mystery series *The Ghost and Max Monroe,* the picture book *Over the River and Through the Woods*, and the cover of the forthcoming middle-grade novel *How to Make a Million*. She resides in Calgary, Alberta.

See you soon!

¡Nos vemos pronto!

www.capstonekids.com